Charles Henry Crandall

Wayside Music

Lyrics, Songs and Sonnets

Charles Henry Crandall

Wayside Music
Lyrics, Songs and Sonnets

ISBN/EAN: 9783744782845

Printed in Europe, USA, Canada, Australia, Japan

Cover: Foto ©Andreas Hilbeck / pixelio.de

More available books at **www.hansebooks.com**

WAYSIDE MUSIC

LYRICS, SONGS AND SONNETS

BY

CHARLES H. CRANDALL

G. P. PUTNAM'S SONS

NEW YORK
27 West Twenty-third Street

LONDON
24 Bedford Street, Strand

The Knickerbocker Press

1893

TO MY WIFE,

MARY VERE DAVENPORT.

AS THE GREATER MUST INCLUDE THE LESS, SO THESE FRAGMENTS
OF MY LIFE ARE NATURALLY COMPRISED IN THAT
LARGER UNWRITTEN VOLUME ALREADY
OFFERED TO YOU.

SPRINGDALE, CONN.
Nov. 1, 1893

"IN COVER"

Love, to your arms I bring them and yield them—
In your full charity take them and shield them—
Wood-bird and blue-bird and blithesome canary,
Some that are jocund and some that are chary.
Weary, perhaps, now their wanderings over,
Silent, they muffle their voices in cover;
Yet they but sleep until you shall wake them,
No one beside can so easily make them
Pipe as of old, when, by your gate swinging,
Sight of your face would set them all singing.

The poetry of earth is never dead.

KEATS.

Soft is the music that would charm us ever.

WORDSWORTH.

CONTENTS

LIFE—LOVE—NATURE

vii

IN LIGHTSOME MOOD

ACKNOWLEDGMENTS

———

About three-fourths of the poems in this volume have appeared previously in *The Century, Harper's Monthly, Atlantic Monthly, Lippincott's Magazine, Cosmopolitan Magazine, St. Nicholas, Outing, Frank Leslie's Monthly, Ladies' Home Journal, Magazine of History, Critic, Art Journal, Judge, Christian Union, Independent, Youth's Companion* and the *New York Tribune.* Acknowledgment is hereby made for kind permission to reprint.

LIFE—LOVE—NATURE.

WAYSIDE MUSIC.

THEY stood there in the bleak, cold street,
   Strolling musicians, quaintly dressed,
Who played an old air ; strong and sweet
   It rose and fell and sank to rest.

Yet still my heart, responsive, beat,
   And with my steps I marked the time.
A subtle music moved my feet,
   Like that which makes a poem rhyme.

Likewise to sounds that swiftly flew
   Soldiers in fight have forward pressed,
Still thinking their dead bugler blew
   Because his challenge fired each breast.

Quickly my fancy strayed away
   To youthful dreams too dear to tell,
When joy outlived the longest day
   And grief was but a word to spell !

Then every morning music brought,
　And time with gladness sped along :
No Ariel thought escaped uncaught,
　And every sound was turned to song.

It comes again, the glorious sound,
　Immortal, wonderful and strange !
It wakes my pulses with a bound,
　And sets a step I would not change.

Sweet, o'er the hills that hide my youth,
　I hear the bells of morning chime.
They ring for honor, love and truth,
　And head and heart are keeping time.

THE LITTLE MISSIONARY.

She has met me many mornings
  With the basket on her arm,
  And a certain subtle charm
Coming not from her adornings,
  But the modest light that lies
  Deep within her shaded eyes.

And she carries naught but blessing
  As she journeys up and down,
  Through the never heeding town,
With her looks the ground caressing ;
  Yet I know her steps are bent
  On some task of good intent.

Maiden, though you would not ask it,
  And your modest eyes would wink,
  I will tell you what I think :
Queens might gladly bear your basket
  If they could appear as true
  And as good and sweet as you !

FIELD VIOLETS.

ALMOST smothered in the roses
In the basket on the curb,
Not a hand their charm discloses;
Or but touches to disturb ;
For amid the cultured graces
Of the crystal-sheltered air
Who, in Broadway's stream of faces,
Who will ever think or care
For violets, blue violets,
Common, wild, sweet, meadow violets ?

Ah, that vision of a woman !
Even the gods would turn to view her !
Jove might very well turn human
Just to claim a kinship to her,
As she sweeps with stately measure
To the little wicker mart.
"I will buy,"—such tones of pleasure—
"If with them you will but part,
Some violets, blue violets,
Common, wild, sweet, meadow violets ! "

And the blossoms seem to redden
  As she lays them to her lips,
And their stems with joy to deaden
  At the warmth that meets their tips
In her bosom's fragrant valley
  As they surge along the street,
While the glances on them rally—
  Girl and flowers, sweet and sweet—
    Just violets, blue violets,
Common, wild, sweet, meadow violets!

1*

PICTURES IN AIR.

I.

A LITTLE child with sunny hair
    Drew with his finger in the air
Pictures that none beside could see—
Forts, castles, deeds of chivalry.

As hour by hour he thus would trace,
Plain grew the lineaments of each face ;
The knight, the courser that he rode,
On his transparent canvas glowed !

His gallery held no Claude Lorraines,
No Gifford, with soft, sunset stains,
No Kensett, rich with autumn light,
No Millet, gloaming into night.

Ay, people smiled.   They could not see
The creatures of his reverie.
Content, unconscious, artist rare,
He drew his pictures in the air !

II.

Now Beauty's spirit evanescent
　His manhood charms with fairy power ;
What though he gives pursuit incessant,
　She only grants a smile or flower.

She breaks the bonds of soft illusion
　He weaves to hold her form within,
And smiles to bring his heart confusion
　Who still must woo, but may not win.

Dear Art ! And yet unsatisfying
　For him who Beauty would ensnare !
They who portray her charm undying
　Still " write in water," paint in air.

While they who seek her joys elysian
　Must catch the spirit's fleeting gleam,
Else never know the artist's vision
　Nor see the glory of his dream.

IN HIDDEN WAYS.

STRANGE is it that the sweetest thing
   Forever is the shyest ;
The sweeter song, the swifter wing,
   Ere thou the singer spyest.

The more the fragrance in the rose,
   The more it bends a-blushing ;
And when with love a maiden glows,
   She hides the telltale flushing.

In depths of night, in gloomy mine,
   In wildwood streams—in stories
Of lowly lives, unsung—there shine
   The world's divinest glories.

As low arbutus blossoms rest
   In modesty unbidden,
So man and nature hide their best,
   And God himself is hidden.

EACH DAY.

I WATCH the sun at morning, and it shines with all
    the gladness
  Of the million million happy eyes that greet its glorious
    birth.
I gaze again at evening, and it gives back all the sadness
  Of the million million weary eyes that watch it sink to
    earth.

PATIENCE.

WHEN we look back at close of day,
　　Whether it close in sun or rain,
We yet can say : It is a way
　　We shall not have to walk again.

For should we live a hundred years—
　　A life of praise, a life of blame,
A life of joy, a life of tears—
　　We would not see two days the same.

Out of the vast, eternal store
　　New duties and new joys arise :
Strange clouds of grief shall gloom us o'er,
　　Fresh bursts of hope shall clear the skies.

Each day a gift !　And life is made
　　Only of days, with gulfs between.
To-day a burden !　Quick 't is weighed,
　　And you shall have a day unseen.

Sweet Patience !　Countless angel bands
　　On urgent errands sweep the skies ;
To-day but let me hold thy hands
　　And gaze into thy steadfast eyes.

OCTOBER.

OH, swiftly forward flashed the train,
   And rich the autumn foliage came,
Until it seemed that past the pane
   October flew on wings of flame!

It was a joy to watch the gleam
   Of tender sky and tinted leaf ;
The wind caressed the placid stream—
   It was a day for sweet belief.

The woodbine, like a lover, wound
   The blushing oak with rosy arms ;
The red leaves fluttering o'er the ground,
   Like couriers, spread the Frost's alarms.

And then there came some faces fair
   Of old-time friends that well I knew—
The sumacs, nodding, debonair,
   In schoolgirl hoods of ruddy hue.

The mellow fields of green and gray
   Told of the harvests they had borne ;
Like golden bombs the pumpkins lay
   Amid the tasselled tents of corn.

It was the time when chestnuts fall
   And early morning frosts the grass,
When urchins in the orchards call
   And mock the crows that southward pass.

I mused upon the season's flight
   From northern pines to southern seas,
Leaving a path of color bright
   With gold and scarlet harmonies.

Then Nature like a woman seemed,
   Whose work was done, and now was dressed
In richest robes, and sat and dreamed
   Of maiden fancies long at rest.

And next the landscape seemed to tell
   A tale of life—of mellow age,
Of the rich fruit of doing well,
   And its eternal heritage.

Ah ! could my Autumn be a scene
   As fair as smiled beneath that sun,
With memories, crowding fast between,
   Of kindnesses received and done,—

Then would I watch the glimmering pane,
   Nor wish the fields to farther roam,
Nor would I ask to stop the train
   That daily brought me nearer home.

THE CHRISTMAS GLOW.

I.

HOW well it is that the Christmas-tide
 Comes not when valleys are decked in pride,
When birds are joyous and fields are gay,
But comes when the year is sad and gray;
When the cold wind cuts the wanderer's cheek,
And makes the boughs in the forest creak!

Ah, sad would the winter be,
And dreary for you and me,
Were it not for the Christmas glow
That shines on the fields of snow!

II.

Twine bright leaves for the summer-time past,
But the crown of the year is at the last;
When its passion is ended, its rest begun,
And there 's no bale in the low, bright sun;
While over the snow floats the evergreen's breath
Like a spirit triumphant over death.

Then while we gladly give,
Each Christmas that we live,
We 'll keep in memory alway
The wondrous gift of Christmas Day.

III.

Then wreathe the holly and laurel green,
And let the mistletoe be seen
Where nuts are cracked before the blaze,
And children in the embers gaze ;
While rosy apples heaped up high
And all good cheer is standing by.

Right gladly greet the timid knock !
A mendicant one may not mock,
For in this humble mask
The Saviour now doth ask.

IV.

Remember the manger so cold and bare,
The breath of kine in the chilly air,
And think how the Child, that shivering lay,
Doth warm the hearts of the world to-day !
The great white star that bent to earth
Kindled the Yule log on each hearth.

Sweet on the morning air
Rose the fair young mother's prayer,
And the stars and the shepherds sang,
And the round, blue heavens rang !

v.

Then, children, wake and your carols sing,
And thoughts as sweet as your faces bring,
For hearts would freeze like the old, old year
If the children did not bring them cheer ;
For he who would the Kingdom win
Must be " as a child " to enter in.

Then glad shall the winter be—
Each winter that we see—
While the beautiful Christmas glow
Shall shine o'er the fields of snow !

THREE TREES.

THE pine-tree grew in the wood—
  Tapering straight and high ;
Stately and proud it stood,
  Dark-green against the sky.
Crowded so close it sought the blue
And ever upward it reached and grew.

The oak-tree stood in the field,
  Beneath it dozed the herds ;
It gave to the mower a shield,
  It gave a home to the birds.
Sturdy and broad, it watched the farms—
Its knotted boughs like the mower's arms.

The apple-tree grew by the wall—
  Ugly and crooked and black ;
But it heard the gardener's call
  And the children rode on its back.
It donned in the Spring a sweet, white cap,
And dropped its treasures in Autumn's lap.

" Now, hey," said the pine, for the wood !
  " Come, live with the forest band.
My comrades will do you good,
  And tall and straight you will stand."
So he mocked the wind with merry shout
And threw his cones like coin about.

" Oh, ho," laughed the sturdy oak,
  " The life of the field for me !
I challenge the lightning stroke,
  My branches are broad and free.
Grow tall and slim in the wood if you will.
Give me the sun and a wind-swept hill."

And the apple-tree murmured low :
  " I am neither straight nor strong ;
Crooked my back doth grow
  With bearing its burdens long."
But it dropped its fruit as it dropped a tear,
And reddened the ground with goodly cheer.

And the Lord of the Harvest heard,
  And He said : " I have need for all,
For the bough that shelters a bird,
  For the beam that pillars a hall ;
And grow they straight, or grow they ill,
They grow but to wait their Master's will."

So a ship of the oak was sent
   Far over the waters blue ;
And the pine was the mast that bent
   As over the waves it flew ;
And the ruddy fruit of the apple-tree
Was sent to a starving isle of the sea.

Now the farmer is strong like the oak,
   And the townsman is proud and tall,
And city and field are full of folk,
   But the Lord has need of all ;
And who will be like the apple-tree
That fed the starving isle of the sea ?

OLD TRINITY CHIMES.

UP above the dust and roar
    Hang the holy bells on high.
O'er the city evermore,
    Hour by hour, their voices cry ;
    Teaching how to live and die,
While the ages onward roll.
    List the hymn, O passer-by !
Jesus, lover of my soul.

When the hands are tired of toil,
    When the weary feet would rest,
When the strife and mad turmoil
    Make existence seem a jest :
    Welcome, music, heavenly guest !
Wafting down from out the sky
    Cadence of that sweet request—
Let me to thy bosom fly.

Sound the footsteps fast and loud
    Where the throng for riches lust,
While they trample—foolish crowd—
    Golden moments into dust !

Shall I let them fade and rust,
Quickly loosed from my control?
Give me first a patient trust,
While the billows round me roll.

Hang the holy bells on high,
Far above the dust and heat ;
Though I pass them, heedless, by,
Faithfully they still repeat
Many an admonition sweet
From their station near the sky,
Chanting of a rest complete
While the tempest still is high.

SUNDAY IN WALL STREET.

FROM Broadway to the river's strand
 The street in silence lies,
Old Trinity, an upturned hand,
 Points finger to the skies.

Now swells the invitation sweet
 From the soft-chiding bells,
And footsteps sound in many a street
 Of stony parallels.

No hand or sunlight warms to-day
 The wealth yon buildings hold ;
On yonder steps there sits at play
 A child with hair of gold.

Ah, fateful street ! Thy strife is loud
 When all thy dollars quake,
And from their friction's dust the crowd
 Their various wages take.

But more I love this Sabbath voice
   Whose softer accents say
That higher wealth still moves the choice
   Of men to keep this day ;

That not in vain do Heaven's rifts
   Shine in the children's eyes ;
That not in vain the church-spire lifts
   Its finger to the skies.

IN THE ATELIER.

IN the studio vaulted with azure,
  With the great flood of day streaming through,
With a hundred fair objects about you
  And the work of the master in view,

You lift the poor chisel and praise it?
  And you 're very kind, so to choose;
But still I am only a chisel,
  Dull, ugly and battered with use.

But I like you to praise her, the statue,
  The fair, moulded figure, the grace
Of the drapery dropped from the shoulder,
  And above all the sweet spirit-face.

Yes I 'm glad and I glory whenever
  I can give his ideals to fame
For my master; but then when I fail him,
  I feel I am wholly to blame.

Then go, give your praise to the artist,
  And wonder, when you 're standing by,
Not at fire that I strike in the marble,
  But that which enkindles his eye.

LOOKING FORWARD.

A CLASSIC frieze of godlike forms
    Moves on and on before my gaze,
Their faces set to sun or storms,
    Hands clasped, no traveller stops nor stays.

And so this chain of courier years
    Will bring the race its golden age,
That glimmering hope that onward cheers,
    That glorifies the oldest page ;

Faces that Phidias scarce had wrought,
    Forms that would make a Spartan gaze,
Minds born to sovereignty of thought,
    Hearts tempered in a crucial blaze,

Love on her throne and Self a slave,
    A willing slave ; this life of ours,
Art, Science, borne on one great wave
    To nobler use, diviner powers !

Clasp closer hands, heroic forms !
    Before, behind. Who would not fain
Set faces stern to sun and storms
    To form a link in such a chain !

3   25

WHO 'LL BUY GREATNESS?

(Father Time, Auctioneer.)

WHO will buy Greatness?   Give me a bid!
   Greatness, a jewel that cannot be hid!
Start it at something, don't all speak at once.
You, sir, my man, you don't look like a dunce—
Look at it carefully, turn it around,
Tap on it—what a fine, echoing sound!
What is it, youngster?   Oh, "work," says the boy.
Thousands would give that for such a fine toy.
"Ease," "patience," "sleep"?   Well, that's a begin-
   ning.
Hundreds say "happiness," but they're not winning.
"Books," "statues," "paintings"—I hear it from twenty—
They are too common, you know I have plenty.
"Wealth"?   Well, to you that may mean a great deal.
"Health"?   Ah, now really it seems that you feel!
What is that?   You would be Anarchy's tool?
And you, sir?   For Greatness he'd gladly play fool!
Warriors—statesmen—your blood and your brain?
Come, this won't answer, you must bid again.
What?   Give you Greatness for such a poor store?

You know in your hearts that you think it worth more.
" Life," "friends " and " honor " ?   Oh, that is not dear ;
" Home," " wife " and " children " ?   Come, sir, speak
    up clear.
Going, now—"faith "—" hope "—that 's a bit nigher !
Oh, gentlemen, cannot you go a point higher?
Now, now—you would make an old auctioneer weep.
Just look at it—Greatness—and going so cheap !

You, there, on the edge, now, I just want to ask,
As you go to your lowly and poorly paid task,
Don't *you* want it?   No?   Then to you I will give it.
That 's the only way, friends, you can get it—is, *live it.*

A PARABLE.

I.

A MERRY streamlet flowed along,
  As cheery as a mower's song !
Its face was brave, its waves were bright,
And broke in drops of diamond light.
Over its bosom, all the way,
The blossoms bent in sweet array ;
It gave them kisses, cool and fleet,
Which left them still more pure and sweet !
This traveller was so strong and true
That it would any service do.
Though it enlisted every brook,
It always gave as well as took,
And in its life of gracious giving
It daily grew to greater living.

II.

A pool of water, stagnant, still,
Lay listlessly beneath a hill.
It served no purpose, save to nurse

Vile weeds which made its visage worse ;
For foulness showed upon its face
And beauty shrank from all the place.
On nature's fairness 't was a blot,
A most unwholesome, evil spot,
And all because it idle lay,
Contented in itself, all day !
Supplied by a few little rills,
It locked them up among the hills,
And always asking, never giving,
It daily died and thought it living !

3*

ROLL-CALL.

OVER the waving willows
    And marble stones a-row,
Over the grass-green billows
    Where heroes lie below,
Thrilling the soldiers' pillows,—
    Listen ! the bugles blow !

Where are the forms that rested
    After the twilight fell,
Whose valor and love were tested
    In fire like the fire of hell ?
Where are the men who breasted
    Shivering shot and shell ?

All the old idols broken,
    Safety and ease they spurned.
What shall we tender, for token,
    Hearts that so highly burned ?
Reverently be it spoken :
    Give them the love they earned.

Not till the morn of glory
   Touches each hallowed spot,
Washing their wounds so gory
   Fit for their brighter lot,
Ever shall fade their story
   Though kings be long forgot !

Yet in each banner swelling
   Its folds against the sky,
In every tear-drop welling
   From every patriot eye,
To-day, their vigil telling,
   Each answers : Here am I.

THE RACE.

THE start, the strain, the springing,
    The leap, the flight, the winging!
The roll of footsteps spurning
The footpath toward us turning!
The white goal growing nearer,
The huzzas sounding clearer,
The spurt, the fierce contending—
The rush, the ease, the ending!

The glow of victory feeling,
The sounds of triumph pealing,
The one fair face all beaming,
And dark eyes passion gleaming;
The white breast quickly heaving—
The wreath of her own weaving—
All make us greet our inning
And make the race worth winning!

MAID WITH THE EYES OF NIGHT.

MAID with the eyes of Night,—
   Sweet Night, the mother of Morn,—
How may I read thee aright,
   So to escape thy scorn?
What is it makes thee bright
   When others are weary and worn?
Maid with the eyes of Night—
   Sweet Night, the mother of Morn!

Teach me to open my heart,
   Like thine, to the ocean of blue,
Till the selfish banks fall apart
   And the tide of Love rushes through;
Till the waves of the great Sea dart
   And fill all the channel anew.
Teach me to open my heart,
   Like thine, to the ocean of blue.

IN A DOVE-COTE.

UNHEEDING the world's strange voices,
  We bide in our safe retreat ;
Each in the other rejoices,
  Softly our pledge we repeat :
    To you I 'm true ;
    I too, to you ;
    Then woo anew ;
    I do, I do !

We fly and alight together,
  We kiss, though we may not sing,
And thrill at the touch of a feather
  Or waft of a soft gray wing.
    Art true ?   Art true ?
    Are you ?   Are you ?
    Then woo, then woo !
    I do, I do !

When the Love-Queen tied us together
  And gathered the snowy rein,
She told us, whatever the weather,
  We never must part again.

'T is true, 't is true ;
To me and you ;
Then woo anew ;
I do, I do !

For our creed is plain and single,
 And this we think is best :
Two lives, one love, to mingle,
 Two birds to fill one nest.
 To you I'm true ;
 I too, to you ;
 Then woo anew ;
 I do, I do !

THE FAIR COPY-HOLDER.

YON window frames her like a saint
   Within some old cathedral rare ;
Perhaps she is not quite so quaint,
   And yet I think her full as fair.

All day she scans the written lines,
   Until the last dull proof is ended,
Calling the various words and signs
   By which each error may be mended.

An interceding angel, she,
   'Twixt printer's press and author's pen ;
Perhaps she 'd find some fault in me !
   Say, maiden, can you not read men ?

Methinks 't is time you learned this art
   Which makes the world's wide page read better,
For love needs proving, heart with heart,
   As well as type with written letter.

FAME.

I GAZED upon tall, dusty shelves,
  Where gilded volumes, stiffly standing,
Looked comfortless as we ourselves
  Would be on such a crowded landing ;
  And though so costly and commanding,
I could but say :   What 's in a name ?
  Hid where the bookworm's tooth is branding,
Methinks I do not care for Fame.

I found a woman, unaware,
  A faded scrap-book slowly turning,
Unheeded fell the gold-brown hair,
  Her eyes with gentle light were burning.
  And as they raised in tender yearning,
And soft she breathed a poet's name,
  I realized that I was learning
That after all I cared for Fame.

A LADY IN THE WEST.

BEYOND the sunset, see, she stands
  With eyes agleam with holy light,
With grace from unimagined lands,
  With purpose pure, with beauty bright !
Sink gently, sun, before those eyes,
  And let her dream 't is Paradise.

Beyond the sunset, safe from harm,
  O let her in her musing weave
Some thought of me as dear and warm
  As twilight brought to blushing Eve—
Sweet premonitions of the night,
  Without a longing for the light.

Beyond the sunset now the beams
  Touch all her warm brown hair to gold ;
Methinks I see it as it gleams,
  And quite forget this dark and cold,
And gladly know, in evening's gloom,
  Her westward skies still brightly bloom !

THE TRAIN.

H ARK!
    It comes!
  It hums!
With ear to ground
I catch the sound,
The warning, courier roar
That runs along before.
The pulsing, struggling now is clearer,
The hillsides echo—nearer, nearer—
Till with a rush like fleeing, frightened cattle,
With dust and wind and clang and shriek and rattle,
Passes the Cyclops of the train!
And there 's a fair face at a pane.
Like a piano string
The rails, unburdened, sing;
The white smoke flies
Up to the skies;
The sound
Is drowned.
Hark!

WISTARIA.

THE standard-bearer of the Spring,
  I mark your conquest of the leas,
As with courageous front you fling
  Your graceful pennons to the breeze.

If lawn or garden chance to show
  Unsightly rock or ugly wall,
You seek it out and kinglike throw
  Your royal purple over all.

The boldest lover scarce would climb
  As high as you to lady's bower ;
Yet, bending low, full many a time
  You reach a little child a flower !

The south wind bears your conquering train
  Of perfume over towns and farms ;
Your couriers are the sun and rain,
  The bumble-bees your knights-at-arms.

Each year your sweet invasion brings
  The memories of long ago,
Yet through a thousand future Springs
  Your flags shall wave, your trumpets blow.

QUATRAINS.

WITH MRS. CRAIK'S POEMS.

DIAMOND, ruby, amethyst, pearl,—
    A woman's gift to you, my girl;
So rich, so rare, whene'er you string them
Forget how poor am I who bring them.

THE CLIFF WALK, NEWPORT.

Those princely homes with flowers and stretching lea
But emphasize the beauty of the sea;
Like some great book whose ocean vistas smile
Whene'er we turn its covers—like a stile!

AT WASHINGTON.

Great avenues that lead from dome to dome
The loyal pilgrims to their nation's home;
Yet over all a glamour like a veil—
The patriot's name that makes its other glories pale.

COMPENSATION.

One loving word from tongue or pen,
    To lift our lives above their sighing,
Is worth a world of weeping when
    Our lips are hushed beyond replying.

CRADLE SONG.

*S*WISH *and swing ! Swish and swing !* Through the
    yellow grain
Stoutly moves the cradler to a low refrain,
While the swaying blades of wheat tremble to his sweep
Till he lays them carefully in a row to sleep ;
  And he feels a mystic rhyme
  Makes his cradle swing in time
    To the rocking of the baby by the door.

Swish and swing ! Swish and swing ! So the cheeks grow
    red ;
Bowls are filled with porridge, and ovens piled with
    bread ;
Bossy claims the middlings, and coltie eats the bran ;
Chicky gets the screenings, and birdie all he can.
  So the cradle's harvest rhyme
  Keeps the reaper's stroke in time
    With the cradle that is rocking by the door.

Thus the golden harvest falls to yield the precious
    wheat.
Life is golden, too, alas ! but only love is sweet.

Labor for the fireside is the royal crown to wear,
And Love that gave the harvest will give each heart its
     share,
  While the reaper swings in time,
  Like a loving, tender rhyme,
    To the rocking of the cradle by the door.

Swish and swing ! Swish and swing ! Ah, the good old
     sound,
Harvest note of gladness all the world around !
Hear the cradles glancing on the hilly steep ;
Hear the little rocker where baby lies asleep—
  Gentle, universal rhyme
  Of the reaper keeping time
    With the rocking of the cradle by the door.

THOMAS'S BATON.

FRAIL bridge, that joins the viewless lands
　　Of silence and of sound ;
Mute summoner, at whose commands
　　The hours with joy are crowned ;
While Harmony, with flower-filled hands,
　　Floats like an angel round !

Or is thy sweep like scythes that play
　　When all the meadows ring,
And dying blade and blossom gay
　　Give sweetest offering ?
So sweetness springs when thou dost sway
　　Each voice and trembling string.

Thine, too, the genius of the rod
　　That cleft the sea in twain
When Israel walked between, dryshod,
　　And all her foes were slain :
Care-freed, we walk the way she trod,
　　Through music's conquered main !

Strange wand, with wondrous power imbued,
 Teach me thy magic ways;
Serve mine, as thy great master's, mood,
 And sounds of Heaven raise!
I take thee up, thou art but wood,
 And mockest at my praise.

THE HARBOR LIGHT.

I.

SEEKING the harbor's gate
 In the dark night and late,
Beating against the wind
And dashing waves that blind,
One hope the pilot cheers
As wearily he nears
The noble, land-locked bay :
That now, with steady ray,
Shines out, serene and far—
A homeward-beckoning star—
 The Harbor Light.

II.

Through what unmeasured miles,
Past what unnumbered isles,
Must we still sail or drift ·
In calms or tempest swift?
How often shall we find
Our reckoning false and blind?
How often at us stare
Wild Hunger, Thirst, Despair !
Yet, o'er the unknown miles,
Still beckons, cheers and smiles
 The Harbor Light.

A PICTURE.

HOW can I paint a face that is so fair
    That none may know its grace until they see it?
Yet should you dream of any face so rare
    It seemed all goodness, that would surely be it.

No bright-eyed girl, although she once was such,
    Is she I sing.   Time her girl-beauty stole,
And since has drawn with soft artistic touch
    The wrinkles that reveal her gentle soul.

Kind charity—which seems almost to cheat
    Her hate of sin by loving still the sinner—
Beams from her eyes, gray eyes, that, though so sweet,
    Scarce hint the depths of tenderness within her.

She always sees some good in every one,—
    And all are glad for this to be her debtor ;
Her coming brings the radiance of the sun,
    And yet she hardly knows she makes us better.

Kind, sympathetic face ! In smiles or tears,
  I cannot see such good in any other,
Nor better tell the tie that so endears
  Than just to write her name, and that is—Mother.

And so with silver cord that naught can sever,
  And set in my unworthy frame of rhyme,
Praying that God may keep it bright forever,
  I hang her picture on the walls of Time.

TO E. C. S.

(On reading " The Nature and Elements of Poetry.")

OUR Critic-Poet ! Who shall henceforth say
⠀⠀That Poetry has fled—an unknown way ?
When Philistines declare the Muse is dead
You point to skies all radiant, overhead ;
And if 't is needful, to convince some fool,
Bring out the scales, the crucible and rule !
On pleasant terms the Scientist you meet ;
Mount up on wings instead of measuring feet ;
Show how the blood in poets' hearts doth spring
And lilt so gladly they are bound to sing ;
Trace the great epic lines of Earth and Time
And find the universe is writ in rhyme.
Yet when you 're through with arguing the case—
When for the flower is wrought the precious vase—
When we are schooled to know a perfect art,
Grant us, once more, a song to thrill the heart !
Then strike the harp, whose strings so fine and clear,
Give us the final proof we love to hear ;
One noble verse shall prove the rabble wrong,
And add new laurels to immortal Song.

TO J. C. R. D.

AS he who tills another's acres leaves
    To the rich owner half the golden sheaves,
So would I share, with gratitude, the yield
Of grace and solace from thy " Fallow Field."

EMERSON.

SHALL that fine face be vainly sought,
　　The brightest of the poet brothers,
The plowshare of whose shining thought
　　Broke such a fertile way for others?

When the old bell his good years rang,
　　Musketaquit, where journeyed he?
Alas, the sister stream he sang
　　Has borne him to a calmer sea.

On Walden pond the ripples flow,
　　And Sleepy Hollow will not wake,
While old Monadnock looks below,
　　Serene as when its poet spake.

May not their calm content declare
　　They still can see him in his haunts,
Or have they learned his lesson rare—
　　" The silent organ loudest chants " ?

Enough that when we leave the marts
    To seek the wealth unfound in strife,
We need not look beyond our hearts
    To find the influence of his life.

From scenes of noise and turmoil shrinking,
    To homely fields his fame he brought.
Life seemed to him worth deepest thinking ;
    So, for the thoughtless crowd, he thought !

ON SUNSET RIDGE.

ON sunset ridge my lady sleeps.
　　As nightly sweeps
The shadow-throng from out the east,
All hushing—man and bird and beast—
And stars of night
Begin to light—
The gems of that far canopy,
The great, blue, upper-world of sky—
I think their million rays have wrought
Some secret entrance to her thought,
And through it shining,
Each night refining,
Make her so like the light that doth endure,
So fresh, so dear, so bright, so true, so pure!
Even as the heavens seem to gently bend
These homestead acres to their skyey trend,
Curving the fields up to a swelling dome,
Lifting to Eden-views the human home,
So, too, that vault of blue
Invites and moulds more true,
Like to itself, as if it were a part,
Her own unchanging, strong, transparent heart.

On sunset ridge there shines a light.
In day or night
I shall not look for it in vain ;
Love's beacon braves the wind and rain,
Nor is there dark
Can dim that mark
To one storm-driven, homeward bark.
How love can beautify the ground !
Or make the solemn heavens around,
Or hills, or trees, or murmuring sea,
All seem a part of home, of thee !
The sweet, good mother,
And sire, and brother,
And she, the friend and sister, sister-friend,
All borrow from the light that thou dost lend.

O long and often may their footsteps tend
Up to those fields where precious memories sleep,
Up to those halls where sons and daughters keep
Old faith, old love, old hope in man's career,
Like old wine, in stout hearts, for others' cheer !
Long may the hilltop light salute the town,
With bright reminder of its old renown !
Long may its sons and daughters sleep and wake
While beauteous suns shall daily set or break
On sunset ridge.

"KEEP TO THE RIGHT."

" KEEP to the right and keep moving," it said,—
The little white card, like a stone for the dead,
The dead who but yesterday, 'neath a blue sky,
Heard laughter and jest drown their muffled death-cry.

Then it sang in the wind and was lisped by the river,
And the words in the wires of the bridge seemed to
      quiver,
And it gleamed in the stars as if nature were proving
The motto of "Keep to the right and keep moving."

Keep to the right and keep moving through life,
Remember there's nothing so needless as strife :
Thus the words of the warning sound clear in the air
As I haste to the heart that I love over there.

A pathway is hung o'er an untravelled river,
It reaches from now to the ever and ever,
And the night hears my wonder, my question, my
      prayer,—
Will I meet with the heart that I love over there?

55

WRITTEN ON A SEASHELL.

FROM yonder sailor on the foam
   The sea some mystery still doth keep ;
From him who makes the hills his home
Some mountain's secret hideth deep.
But where the land and billows meet
Each unto each their tales repeat.
The breakers roar : *Forevermore !*
Forevermore ! replies the shore.
And listening here, there rises clear
The sweet, sad music of the sphere :
Hearts, like the billows, throbbing, breaking ;
Love, like the echoes, dying, waking !

WELCOME.

C. L. K.

WELCOME from absence all too long,
  Singer, whose name with music thrills !
Welcome, the voice whose silver song
  Has lately linked all Europe's hills !

We wait, as Spring waits for the birds,
  Until again thy voice we hear,
Wedded to soft Italian words,
  Or homelike melodies more dear.

Gaze on familiar field and lake,—
  Let every mountain, stream and bay
Thy memory to music wake,
  Like robins that return in May.

America is proud of thee,
  Her singer, and though far above
Our praises thy deserving be,
  There 's nothing yet too high to love !

"FOR POETS ONLY."

" A POET for poets." 'T was said, years ago,
When his fame first arose in the East—even so.
But the ranks of the poets soon multiplied fast—
The poets who read—and 't was said at the last,
When his books sold by thousands when damp from the
      press :—
" It 's worth while to write just for poets, we guess ! "

A poet for poets ! Well, how could there be
An artist to any who Art could not see ?
Can loveliest stanza enrapture the ear
Unless one shall first be a poet to hear ?
Go, ask any bard in the East or the West,
Is praise from a poet not always the best ?

" Ah, we know what you mean—silent poets—the throng
Who drink in the music but utter no song ! "
They are poets, in truth, yet I love the heart-glow
Of those who have served at the altar, who know
The thrill and the yearning, when, in the still night,
A whisper-voice tells them to rise and to write.

SARATOGA.

(Written for the Dedication of the Battle Monument at Schuylersville, N. Y.)

HISTORIC Hudson! Haste not by to-day!
    More gently let thy waters take their way,
     As on thy banks we dedicate
     This shaft unto the dead, the great,
Whose memory, like thy stream, a shining story,
Shall broaden to a boundless sea of glory.

The dwellers in Manhattan's crowded mart
May here see Nature play her silent part.
     The stream that brings them wealth
     Here steps with bashful stealth,
Soft, as in moccasins an Indian maiden,
Its breast with trees, like tresses, overladen.

As now from many a path in life you meet,
The hills in their immortal verdure greet,
     Come with me in my boat of rhyme,
     Come and ascend the stream of time,
Back when the nation was a century newer
And held true heroes, though her sons were fewer.

Quiet for many a year has here been found—
The wild bird feared no martial sight nor sound.
  Under the peaceful fields, well-kept,
  The ashes of the soldier slept,
With summer's guard of tasselled corn around,
And winter's snow-shroud hallowing the ground.

On yonder plain, where Burgoyne's grenadiers
Laid down the arms they loved, with bitter tears,
  The armies of the grass and grain
  Have struggled o'er and o'er again,
In changing regiments of green and yellow,
Through lusty June, through August, ripe and mellow.

 . . . .

Honor the past! Already has there flown
From Saratoga and from Horicon
  All but their names—whose gentle sounds
  Still linger round the burial mounds—
Of that dark race, which, ever westward flying,
Now, like a sunset's light, is slowly dying.

The modern spirit would itself demean
Did we not flock, to-day, to such a scene;
  For from the nation's rugged past,
  The rude days when her fate was cast,
Has flowed the stream that makes all men draw near her,
The Freedom that has made the world revere her.

Here fell the blow that made oppression reel,
And set on Freedom's cause its brightest seal.
  Honor to Schuyler, Morgan, Gates,
  The victors over threatening fates,
And praise for him whose niche has but a name,
Too valiant to forget, too base for fame !

Honor to every nameless, fallen one !
Honor them all, each one the country's son !
  Stone for their fitting monument
  From many a State has here been sent,
And every block that lifts its tapering spire
Is sacred as if touched with holy fire.

First on this soil the flag we love to name
Flew in the wind, a never-dying flame !
  Giving a heart-beat to the land,
  Binding it with a silken band—
An amulet where'er its name is spoken—
'Gainst which no sword shall ever fall unbroken !
  .   .   .   .

And when this ceremonial pomp shall pass,
And undisturbed shall glow and fade the grass,
  While storm and sun and shadow chase
  Across each bronze, stern-featured face,
Yet shall this place to many a one be dear ;
And Liberty shall love to linger here !

6

To multitudes who come with pilgrim feet
The sculptured tablets will their tales repeat :
   Again in fancy will be seen
   The redcoats on the meadows green,
And Jane McCrea shall leave her pillow gory,
Or hearts be moved by Lady Acland's story.

For she whose love was greater than her fears,
Who sought our camp and conquered it with tears,
   Was but a type of woman's heart—
   Which ever bravely plays its part—
Which soothes in peace, in war gives cheering word,
Melts lead to ball and reaches down the sword !

Long may our tribute to the brave endure,
Here where the winds and waters journey pure,
   And give to all who on it gaze
   The spirit of those olden days,
When love of right and liberty unbound
The strongest clasp that loved ones threw around.

Speak ! Sons of Saratoga here to-day!
Shall it not be this valley's boast to say :
   The soil of Saratoga sends
   The kind of man that never bends,
Whether in council hall a vote he wield
Or grasps a gun upon a battlefield ?

And you, fair village, with your skyward spires,
Your leisurely canal, your factory fires,
   Keep for yourself as fair a fame
   As his, who gave to you a name—
The courtly, soldier-gentleman who now,
Kindly in bronze, meets you with open brow.
.   .   .   .

England ! a foe no longer, peace to thee !
A common lineage throbs beneath the sea ;
   And though this day brings nearer heart
   The nation's friends who took our part,
We send to her who rules thy fair demesnes
Greeting from sixty million kings and queens !

The nation that forgets its Marathon
Has lost the choicest glory it has won.
   Then let this granite shaft of grace
   Forever be a rallying-place
For liberty and honor, till the day
The stone is dust, the river dried away !

And when, a century hence, this column hath
Whirled with the world through space its spiral path,
   And men of grander, later days,
   With faces strange, upon it gaze ;
'T will draw our thought, like lightning from the skies :
The man who dies for country never dies !

DIONDEHOWA RIVER.

I.

LATE the sun had left the heavens, day into the night
    was flowing,
As I wandered through the meadow to the hollow 'neath
    the hill ;
Where the never-resting river ever murmurs in its going,
Charming all its way with music as it journeys to the
    mill.

Pausing then a while to listen to its sad and mystic singing,
Wonder stole me and the moment seemed to thrill with
    meaning strange ;
For the rushing of the river seemed a voice forever
    ringing
Deepest truths of human destiny and thoughts beyond
    my range.

Softly then I trod the margin as I stole down near and
    nearer,
Holding to the willow branches as I bent down to the
    wave ;

While a voice rose through the water with a silver ca-
dence clearer
Than was ever heard by Triton in his starry ocean
cave !

Long I listened to the quiring of this nymph that sang so
sweetly
That she burdened all the valley from the mountains to
the sea.
And she spoke a subtle language, that enchanted me
completely,
This is but a feeble echo of the song she sang to me :

SONG.

" *Willows, bending o'er my shallows, nesting birds that sing
above me,*
*Sedgy marshes fringing round me, rocks that frown upon
my way ;*
*Stars that gaze upon my bosom, trembling as if you did
love me,*
Look with pity on my fortune, list with pity to my lay.

" *For the fleet sun hath outrun me, and the day hath gone
and left me,*
*And the night-winds come on quickly, stealing down into the
vale ;*
6*

All my gladness, all my laughter, all my beauty is bereft
　me,
While the shores hold frightful shadows, and the trees
　groan in the gale.

" Still I hurry blindly onward, and a distant roaring tells
　me
I am coming to the cataract, I hear its awful moan ;
Yet I cannot pause a moment for a mystic power compels
　me,
Ever tearing me away whene'er I cling around a stone.

" O ye forests and ye night-winds, and ye birds above me
　dreaming,
And ye stars that shine so tenderly, as always ye have
　shone,
Pity her who wanders darkly with no sunlight on her
　streaming,
Pity her who journeys sadly through the gloomy night
　alone."

II.

Day had raised its golden sceptre, and the sun was gayly
　riding
With tidings from the eastern seas to mountains in the
　west,

When again I crossed the meadow to the river calmly
    gliding
On its now apparent mission, to its long eternal rest.

For it hasted gayly onward and it laughed at all de-
    tainers,
As it sped o'er shining shallows, as it rippled o'er the
    stones ;
And it served all men with patience, caring not if they
    were gainers,
Only bound to blend its music with the ocean's organ-tones

Joyously the waves leapt forward, flowers upon their
    bosoms floating,
Birds sang flying o'er its surface, willows trembled with
    delight ;
Beauty was so glad about me I had near forgotten noting
If I still might hear the singing of the naiad of the night.

Then I listened for the music while the shadows slowly
    shifted,
Till I slept beside the waters, drowsiness had changed to
    dream ;
When again arose the voice, as if the river's heart was
    rifted !
O that I might sing the words as did the spirit of the
    stream.

SONG.

"*Gladly, gladly I am gliding, fearing naught of ill or sorrow,*
Now that light doth lead me on I see the grandeur of the way ;
Tell me not that night will darken, tell me not of a to-morrow,
Till I have fulfilled the duty and the mission of to-day.

"*Fare ye well, my native mountains, from your bosoms ye*
　　have fed me,
Memory shall hold you dearest of the treasures she has won ;
But I would not tarry longer, not in vain the Hand hath
　　led me,
Work is waiting for my effort, nature needs me further on.

"*O how sweet to trust completely that the best is still be-*
　　fore us,
Letting all our life run forward with a faith that naught
　　can foil,
Knowing that the stars and blossoms and the holy angels
　　o'er us
Are but brighter shining comrades in love's brotherhood of
　　toil !

"*As the channel widens, deepens, I am charmed by higher*
　　beauty,
In the bearing others' burdens, making others' sorrows mine ;
Joyfully my current rushes 'twixt the guiding banks of duty,
And, thou ocean, gladly will I lose my little life in thine."

IN LIGHTSOME MOOD.

AT FIRST SIGHT.

HAST thou a heart, O deep-eyed girl,
　　To match that glance of thine?
Hast thou a soul as rich and sweet,
　　And may I call it mine?

I have no heart, O blue-eyed boy,
　　I am a maid forlorn;
For I dreamed of you and lost my heart
　　Long years ere I was born.

I have thy heart, O dark-eyed maid,
　　And hard within my breast
It leaps to meet its owner sweet
　　That it may be at rest.

And I have thine, O fair-eyed lad,
　　It flutters like a feather.
Then, since they may not be exchanged,
　　Let's keep them close together!

69

ON MARY'S FAIRNESS.

(*Imitation of Herrick.*)

FEW are the sights so fair
  As Mary when she goes
Out in the morning air
  To pluck a dewy rose.

Then at her table-tasks
  She looks so sweet and wise,
It seems to me she asks
  A blessing with her eyes.

But she may look most fair,
  My fancy hath confest,
When, hiding in her hair,
  She lays her down to rest.

Whether she combs her curls,
  Or smiles, or smells her rose,
She is the queen of girls—
  And that, perhaps, she knows!

HESPERIDES.

O MAIDEN with unclouded brow,
　　Whose thoughts are words too fine to speak,
Come, let thine eyes pour for me now
　　The stream that hides the pearls I seek !

Then will I search its depths, and string
　　An amulet to set us free,
To seek the clime where naught can bring
　　A feeble counterfeit of thee.

I know the way to Love's own land ;
　　I told the rose to scent the gales ;
A dream shall bear us to its strand,
　　And Fancy tend the shining sails.

It rises fair, the Isle of Bliss,
　　Where Love and Thought shall be our slaves,
And each uncounted smile and kiss
　　Shall come and go like summer waves.

Come, love, our vessel frets the sand,
　　That waits impatient for thy feet ;
A quiet walk, a yielded hand—
　　And now we know that life is sweet.

A PERFECT HEART.

A PERFECT heart.   Ah, tell me where
   This jewel lies that I would wear.
   If in your breast it be not found
   I will not look in other ground,
But yield me up to my despair.
   So many hearts, the world around,
   Yield to the touch a hollow sound,
I feel that I shall never snare
         A perfect heart.

I will not search in upper air
If yours be not beyond compare,
   Yet mine with yours would fain be bound.
Perhaps the two, in union crowned,
Might form that wonder, sweet and rare,
         A perfect heart.

COMMUNICATION.

A S trees that many a vale and hill
　　Divide, yet, standing by one stream,
　May, through its subtle current, seem
To hold communication still ;

So, Friend, my thought flows fast and free,
　A constant current none may note,
　Except when on its flood I float
A letter, like a leaf, to thee.

NEEDLESS.

THERE is no need for me to tell
　　What blossom has the happy lot
To match the eyes whose glances spell :
　　Forget-me-not.

And as they cannot but succeed
　　In that remembrance which they plot,
I see no need for them to plead :
　　Forget-me-not !

TO A BEAUTY.

WHEN we pass by a flower on our way
  Does it matter at all if we say
    It is winsome and fair
    And it perfumes the air
And its beauty enriches the day ?

No, a rose is a rose just the same,
Though we give it our praise or our blame ;
    For its charm is complete,
    And it lives to be sweet,
Like a lady I need not to name !

So a wish and a blessing I send her,
May the angels and fairies attend her,
    And turn every dart
    In her journey apart,
With her beauty alone to defend her.

THE GOLDEN AGE.

M Y love and I laugh o'er the page
⠀⠀That tells the varied story
How love ran in the Golden Age—
⠀⠀We care not for its glory.

Idly we read how earthly maids
⠀⠀Entangled Jove, the mighty,
Or how Adonis in the glades
⠀⠀Played with fair Aphrodite.

Pan the sweet river-nymph may woo,
⠀⠀Pygmalion, Galatea ;
Our love is just as sweet and true
⠀⠀As theirs by blue Ægea.

Nor lacks it the enchanting power
⠀⠀That blends divine with human ;
My love will change at any hour
⠀⠀To goddess or to woman !

Thus love's eternal heritage
⠀⠀Illumes our modern portals.
Cupid and Psyche know not age,
⠀⠀And we, too, are immortals.

BY THE BROOK.

MY life dates newly from a look
    That lit the gem of Memory's hours
The day we wandered up the brook
    In quest of summer flowers.

We stood a little way apart
    Upon a shady, grassy rise,
When all the beauty of your heart
    Came rushing to your eyes ;

A look so full of trust and truth,
    Transparent, pure as virgin gold,
It spoke more eloquence, in sooth,
    Than tongue could e'er have told.

And yet, my love, if e'er by chance,
    You learn the language of the birds,
Then tell the message of that glance
    In sweet, unworldly words.

AN OCTOBER BIRTHDAY.

O GENTLE maid, whose charms outshine
    The queenly month that bore thee,
Look kindly on these gifts of mine
    That now I lay before thee.

Here 're chestnuts ! Not the ancient puns
    That make one sad and sober,
But nuts that ripened in the suns
    Of your own bright October.

The very color of your eyes
    Their glossy shells are sporting ;
Their burr a heart that open flies
    When bold Jack Frost is courting.

Who would not brave the wildest sea
    In such well-armored vessel,
Or even wish a nut to be
    In such a spot to nestle !

As for these late blue flowers, I wot
    Your glances, far from cruel,
Will make each a forget-me-not,
    And so a fadeless jewel.

78

A MASQUE OF SINGERS.

The silent concert hall, the empty stage and dark,
And has their music vanished? Heart and memory, hark!

A. P. AND S. S.

O BRING again the brightness and the glory,
  The haunting rapture of the "Trovatore";—
They, the two artists, striving for the prize,
Winging their voices up to Verdi's skies!

C. N.

A voice so lovely and a form so queenly,
And yet the world lets you sing on serenely!
I would not think a king would be deterred
From risking empires to cage such a bird!

E. T.

Moore's gem beneath her vocal genius glows,—
Upon her breast a scarlet-petalled rose!
Which swelled more sweetly as her voice out-rang,
The rose she wore, or the "Last Rose" she sang?

H. M. S.

She but a girl, that fountain, music playing?
Yet there are fairy forces round her straying ;
Something of bird and something more than woman,
Let me believe her more than simply human !

A MASQUE OF POETS.

Lifting a leaflet to their air I drew
Their love and Godspeed, kindly as the dew.

D. M. C.

SHE who wrote " Philip," tenderest of songs,
    And nobly interwove on fiction's page
Wise woman-counsel, worthy of a sage,
With honest love that now her fame prolongs.

L. M. A.

This one, demure as if in Sister's hood,
Hid her ambition in her tales for good.
But round her how the children's faces shine—
Madonna-like—an aurole divine !

M. M. D.

For songs, like blossoms, strewn " along the way,"
For tales that make us youthful all the day,
For these must rise an incense of the heart,
And reach thee, always, whereso'er thou art.

E. M. H.

Something of wildwood grace her figure thrills—
Shy as arbutus on her native hills,—
But ask me not to paint such winsome grace—
A muse who smiles and banters face to face!

A MASQUE OF BEAUTIES.

Who tires, at last, in following Beauty's track,
Must needs send Memory to bring her back.

M. A. N.

A STATUE ? No, for even now she stirred,
And turned that poisèd head, so like a bird.
The public her Pygmalion was.   To-day
It mourns its Galatea, stolen away !

L. L.

By me she watches, with a throbbing heart,
The flames consume the temple of her Art,
While flushes with her lily features toy :—
The face of Helen at the siege of Troy !

B. C.

A brave, bright girl, who will not comprehend
The world was made for aught but Pleasure's end ;
Who 'd walk up to the gates of Paradise
And challenge Peter to withstand her eyes.

C. U. P.

Her eyes are as opals that cannot look sober,
Beware them unless you were born in October,
For men would be exiles could they but be bound
In the gold tresses wherewith she is crowned.

SONGS.

THE HAPPY FARMER.

(Suggested by the music, " The Happy Farmer," by Robert Schumann.)

I.

(Andante.)

O'ER mountain peaks the morning breaks,
    The robin at my window wakes,
And calls me now to guide the plow
Down where the waving willows bow.
My sturdy team goes swiftly round
And swiftly turns the fragrant ground,
While breezes blow and grasses grow,
And birds of passage northward go.
    Fly on, swift birds, across the land !
    And blow, ye winds, from strand to strand !
    For well I know, where'er ye go,
    Ye see no happier man below,
    For my heart is light and my love is true,
    And the day is full of work to do !

II.

(*Adagio.*)

The plow is still and blushes fill
The heavens o'er the western hill,
As homeward now, with tossing mane,
My steeds go stepping down the lane.
How glad they reach the water-trough !
And grateful now, with harness off,
They follow to the pasture ground,
And break away with playful bound.
    Now softly fall the meadow bars,
    And silently steal out the stars,
    And as I watch the splendid night
    I hear a footstep falling light,
    And some one saying, sweet and true,
    " Come, love, there 's no more work to do ! "

"ROBIN ADAIR."

(Written for the music.)

PLAINTIVE the song I heard
   In the still night,
Like to a morning bird
   Longing for light.
     For 't was a maiden's song—
     Waiting her lover long—
     Still singing sweet and strong :
      Robin Adair.

Close to the window-seat
   Softly I stole,
Wond'ring who sang so sweet
   Out of her soul.
     My own love did I see,
     Looking so wistfully,
     While she sang tenderly :
      Robin Adair.

Into my arms she sprang,
   White as a dove ;
Forgot the song she sang,
   All but her love !

Brightest of earthly things—
Memories that music brings,
When now with me she sings :
    Robin Adair.

NEVER FEAR.

I HAVE no fear for my fair, fair ship,
  Wherever her course may lay,
For her sails are white in the morning light,
  And her captain knows the way.

On the rolling tide she will lightly glide,
  Like a bird that is homeward winging,
Like a loving thought to the right one brought
  That needs not any bringing !

She will safely sail to her harbor home,
  For the winds and the waters love her ;
So I have no fear, wherever she steer
  With the good bright stars above her.

JUNE SONG.

OH sing of a scudding sky in June,
  When the air is fresh and sweet,
When the yachts of God are all abroad—
  Ten million in a fleet;
Nor mightiest hand in all the land
  Can stay one snowy sheet !

The oriole and the bobolink
  Fling challenge to the quail ;
The clover nods to the milk-weed pods
  And the daisies dot the swale ;
The soul of the rose on light wing goes,
  And sweetens all the gale.

Ah, fair is the green world underneath,
  But oh, for the blue above !
To leave the grass and lightly pass
  As the pinion of a dove
To the snowy boat that seems to float
  To the haven of my love !

Then sing of a scudding sky in June,
  When the world is fresh and sweet ;
When the yachts of God are all abroad,—
  Ten million in the fleet ;
Nor mightiest hand in all the land
  Can furl one flying sheet.

ONE LITTLE ROOM.

ONE little room, with thee, my love,
    Is large enough for me ;
It were as good as all the world
    If only it held thee.
Our little hut, in sun or shade,
    Might stand on rock or lea ;
I would not covet palaces
    Beside the azure sea.

One little window would suffice,
    If when I came at night
Thy smiling face were waiting there—
    My homeward-beckoning light !
I only ask one lowly door
    And but a glimpse of grass,
If out and in, like angel's feet,
    Thy steps will daily pass.

One little table, just for two,
    One candle in its place,
And lowly fare, so that it drew
    The blessing of thy face.

One little ingle's light should throw
　Its beams about the room,
Although I know thy smile alone
　Would banish all the gloom !

O wind that hurtles from the strand,
　Do me a favor sweet ;
O blow my song across the land
　And lay it at her feet.
And let her know I wait and long
　To throw the world aside
If she will make my hut a heaven
　By coming there to bide.

MY TROUBADOUR.

HIGH in the maple swinging,
   To usher in with singing
The wedding of the dawn
With the dew upon the lawn,
You cheery little poet !
Although you do not know it
And think no one is near you,
We hear you, we hear you !
   Carol on, Carol on !

Hark, in the orchard hidden,
A serenade unbidden !
And by this dainty clue,
Robin, we know it 's you.
No, you cannot deceive us,
Pretending that you leave us !
We found you out, you dear, you !
We hear you, we hear you !
   Carol on, Carol on !

Now on the meadow floor
The scarlet troubadour
Such melody is letting

The sun forgets its setting !
You music-beating heart,
Doing your little part,
You shall be seen and heard
Though you are but a bird !
So never, never fear you ;
We hear you, we hear you !
   Carol on, Carol on!

"DREAMS OF THE PAST."

(Written for the music.)

I.

FAIR dies the sunset, so golden and tender,
  Wistfully charming our spirits away;
So all the gladness or music or sadness,
  All that is beautiful never can stay.
Yet as the sunshine that near us at noonday
  Seemed not so lovable, winsome and dear;
So all the joy and the love and the friendship,
  When far away, more enchanting appear.

II.

They who have labored well love the night's coming,
  Gladly they wait a more beautiful morn.
All of the good we have loved is immortal;
  Out of the sunset the sunrise is born.
When in the twilight we long to look backward,
  Then, oh, come back again, lovely and clear,
Sweet as a sunrise that brightens forever,
  Dreams of the past, once again, oh, appear!

WILLOW SONG.

WILLOW, reaching to the water
 Loving arms to hold it back,
Art thou patient with thy fortune?
 Does thy life know any lack?

Art thou mindful that the streamlet
 Ripples, laughs, and fleets away?
Wilt thou woo it thus forever,
 Constant ever to it stay?

Shaking then its head so hoary
 With a hundred years, it said:
Though 't is fickle I am faithful,
 Love is life till life is dead.

Willow, Willow, we are brothers;
 I am wooing, like to thee,
One as fickle as thy river,
 Who but flouts and laughs at me!

SKATING SONG.

COME, while the north wind sings !
 We 'll change our feet for wings,
 As like a lance
 We glide and glance,
And loud the good steel rings.

Fleet Mercury and Mars
And all the other stars,
 Companions bright,
 Will lend a light
That 's fit for kings and czars.

Now merry girls are whist
As words of love they list,
 And cheeks burn red
 As if they said :
We 're waiting to be kissed !

A SONG FOR THE HICKORY TREE.

I.

A SONG for the hickory tree !
   While the wind is blowing free,
And the golden leaves and silver nuts
Drop down for you and me !

As we pull the nuggets out
From their crypts with merry shout,
   The air is filled with a scent distilled
Like the spices of the South.

A health for the hickory tree—
Rough-coated, hale and free—
   For its flesh is white and its heart is bright,
And it laughs with you and me !

II.

The squirrel says with a wink,
"I'd sing a song, I think,
   To the girl who stands with snow-white hands
And eyes that flash and blink.

"Whose flesh is white and strong,
Whose heart is free from wrong,
    And sound and sweet as the nut at her feet,
And better than any song."

So, take the song, my queen,
For a kiss and a philopene !
    'Mid the golden leaves and silver nuts,
I kneel on the carpet green.

BREAK BRIGHTLY,
GLORIOUS EASTER MORN.

BREAK brightly, glorious Easter morn,
   Now that the winter snows have fled,
And so deny with splendid scorn
   That earth is haggard, old and dead!

A million million emerald spears
   Rise to proclaim her ever young,
And hark! Her ever youthful years
   On lily bells are sweetly rung.

Oh, freely swing and grandly swell,
   Ye church-tower bells, with merry din;
The darkness of our souls expel
   And let the light of love come in.

Break brightly, glorious Easter morn,
   Into these gloomy hearts of ours,
That they, too, may this day adorn,
   And shed a perfume like the flowers.

SONNETS.

THE OLD DWELLING.

SEE how the dwelling trembles to its fall—
　　The wondrous house of life now leased to death ;
　How softly in and out moves the light breath,
And gently in the tender-memoried hall
Speaks the loved owner, soon beyond recall.
　In the fast-closing windows glimmereth
　A dying glory as when sunset saith
Good-night, sweet dreams, and faith and hope to all.

Thus, full of enterprise and joyous trust,
　　Perched on a sill, serene and plumed for flight,
　　A dove will pause, while ruin round it lies.
So, too, dear soul, although thy house is dust,
　　Yet thou, thyself, now free as morning light,
　　　Canst find another home, 'neath other skies.

THE HUMAN PLAN.

CHILD, weary of thy baubles of to-day—
    Child with the golden or the silver hair—
  Say, how would'st thou have built creation's stair,
Had'st thou been free to have thy puny way?
Could thy intelligence have shot the ray
    That lit the universe of upper air?
  Would'st thou have bid the surging stars to dare
Their glorious flight and never stop nor stay?

Yet, casting on this life thy weak disdain,
    Thou triest to guess thy lot in loftier places,
      To draw the heaven of our human need;
A door of Rest, a flash of wings, a strain
    Of 'trancing music, and the long-lost faces!
      But, after all, what may be Heaven indeed?

WOMAN.

FAIRER than all the fantasies that dart
 Adown the dreams of our most favored sleep,
 Thy lovely form since Eden's day doth keep
The constant pattern of a perfect art !
Yet more do we admire thy better part,
 The spirit strong to smile when others weep ;
 And well know we who sail life's ocean deep
There is no haven like a woman's heart.

Thus, often weary ere the victory 's won,
 Tired with my task, my head I fain would lay
 In some good lady's lap as did the Dane,
And watch the action of the world go on,
 Knowing 't is but a play within a play,
 The fleeting portion of an endless plan.

ILLUSIONS.

THE free, bright gold-mines on the sunset hills—
    The pure, sweet promises that star the stems
  When quick-foot May her emerald garment hems
With apple-blossoms—diamond-shower that fills
Winter with white forgetfulness of ills—
    All cheats ! Gold—dross ! May's—imitation gems !
    And where are all the frail snow diadems
The world has wept away in annual rills ?

Yet has the Hand that framed our stately dwelling
    Hidden in beauty architrave and beam,
Placed no black orbs in hopeless heavens knelling,
    But azure arch with studded stars agleam ;
And spirit voices keep on softly telling
    To doubt the Analyst and trust the Dream.

SLEEP'S CONQUEST.

INVISIBLE armies come, we know not whence,
    And like a still, insinuating tide
Encompass us about on every side.
They overpower each weary, outpost sense
Till thought is taken, sleeping in his tents.
    Yet now the conqueror, with a lofty pride,
    Becomes our guardian, with us doth abide,
And plans all night our wondrous recompense.

He takes away the worn and tarnished day
    And brings to-morrow, bride without a stain ;
    Gives us fresh liberty, a chance to mend—
Life, hope and friends enhanced with fresh array.
    Then, when we fail, he conquers us again,
    Paroling us each day until the end.

THE FOREST KNIGHTS.

NOVEMBER, grizzled bugler, blows his horn
 To call the forest knights from tournament,
 And leafy dalliance with zephyrs spent,
And languorous months that call to them forlorn.
For now the old strength in their breasts is born ;
 Oak, ash and maple, with their great arms bent,
 Fling by their plumes, gay garnitures are rent,
And in their stead a mail of ice is worn.

Ah, sore the dint the forest knights must bear
 When all the wrack of pagan, wintry storms
 From out the North leaps on the noble band !
How arms must strike and clash, and trumpets blare,
 And armor ring, ere once again their forms
 Wear wreaths of victory from Summer's hand !

THE NEW YEAR.

A WANDERING heir to wealth I never piled,
　　I take this gift of Time, and as I hold
This New Year with its counted days of gold,
I muse and wonder like a little child—
Hardly to such rich fortune reconciled—
　　Yet planning how to spend it, and with bold
　　Design to fill each day with manifold
Good deeds, fair thoughts, and pleasures undefiled.

Why should wealth make us spendthrift ?　In one day
　　A man may write a never-dying word,
　　　　Or strike a blow to ring adown the years !
Yet here are thrice a hundred ; and shall they
　　Be doled out like the last, with ill use blurred ?
　　　　O fair New Year ! I take the gift with tears.

COLUMBUS.

(*1893.*)

YOU who are baffled and are sore distraught
　　With long-successive tidal waves of doom,
　Losing each gallant hope in angry boom
Of billows gnashing all your plans to naught ;
Look at this man who lacked all that is taught
　By the late centuries ; who, on the gloom
　Of a sea fury-haunted marked out room
For a great Land that lived in no one's thought !

By the light given, following his star,
　Though lesser men might fear or chide or laugh,
　　He drave ahead ; and when amid his crew
He knelt where now a hundred millions are,
　Gave us a continent, his cenotaph,
　　To tell forever what one man may do.

WRITTEN IN A VOLUME OF SHAKESPEARE.

BETWEEN these covers a fair country lies,
  Which, though much travelled, always seemeth new ;
  Far mountain peaks of Thought reach to the blue,
While placid meadows please less daring eyes.
Deep glens and ivied walls where daylight dies
  Tell of Romance, and lovers brush the dew
  By moonlit stream and lake, while never few
Are the rich bursts of Song that shake the skies.

This country's king holds never-ending court ;
  To him there come from all his wide domain
Minstrels of Love and spangled imps of Sport,
  And messengers of Fancy, Joy and Pain :
Of man and nature he has full report ;
  He made his kingdom, none dispute his reign.

ADELAIDE NEILSON.

A VOICE that mocks a laughing, mountain brook,
   A smile as swift as summer swallows fly,
  And eyes that drain the beauty of the sky
To fill our hearts with but a single look !
But lack of lovely words ! For if I took
   A thousand pages whereupon to try
  To draw her attributes, my pen would dry,
And I would write but " Beauty " in the book.

Yet may be found her spirit masked in flowers,
   Her genius-light in yonder steadfast star,
    Her winsome graces in the wandering stream ;
And from the perfect poet of all hours
   We catch the message, falling from afar :
    " *This Rosalind is worthy of my dream.*"

SUNSET ON THE PALISADES.

GIVE me a golden frame for yonder sky
   And let me hang it on my memory's wall,
That I may not forget how sweetly fall
The mellow hues that seem to sanctify
The purple cliffs, the river, and, more nigh,
   The old, bare elm-tree, with its branches tall
   Etched on the radiance, and yon manor-hall
With gray stone walls whereon the lichens lie.

Now pales the golden zone the world doth wear,
   And, fleck by fleck, the crimson tints retreat
      From Night's gray wings that over me unroll.
Across the hills the feet of Twilight fare,
   While sounds of vesper bells come, low and sweet,
      As if from yonder Evening Star they stole.

TO BEATRICE CAMERON.

(*With "Lady Geraldine's Courtship."*)

FEW things are good enough to give away—
   In friendship's light pure diamonds are cheap—
But kindly deeds and words must ever keep
Their lustre bright, and so to you I say :
Keep this, good heart, in memory of the day
   We watched the busy farmers mow and reap
   Across the stream, or on the hillside steep
The shadows of the clouds in endless play.

Again the scene before me rises clear,
   And you your earnest glances on me bend ;
Soft falls the river's music on my ear,
   The leaves their light, æolian language lend ;
And yet that lovely day is only dear
   Because it framed the picture of my friend.

THE DAWN.

MY day of youth had set in doubt and tears,
    It seemed an endless night encompassed me,
  I faltered on in paths I could not see,
Forgot the music of my morning years
  And fell into the hands of nameless fears,
While clouds rolled over life's once sunny lea.
    Then dawned the day when I won sight of thee,
And, as a man in early dawning hears
The woods and fields in many warblings wake,
  Or as the mere by morning's amulet
Is charmed to glory like a heavenly lake,
  So did my soul awake when first we met,
And life became immortal for thy sake—
  O dearest Love, my sun that shall not set!

OLIVER WENDELL HOLMES.

THOU age-crowned poet, with the smile of youth,
　　Who hast so blent our laughter with our tears,
Thou 'lt ne'er be homeless, for thou hast in truth
　　Leased homes in hearts for many, many years !
Though puzzled by the parson's wondrous "shay,"
　　We cannot miss the logic of thy love,
Which made " Nautilus " sing a deathless lay
　　And " Voiceless " voice so many a songless dove.

Light-hearted singer, happy because pure,
　　Thy books are not for dusty upper shelves,
Because thou hast not writ of things obscure,
　　But sung to us the music of ourselves.
Long may thy " Leaf " cling to the precious bough !
Long may we prize thy songs as we do now !

" H. H."

ABOVE this simple tribute to her worth
   I write the letters she was wont to sign—
  The slender clue to many a lovely line
By her large poet-nature given birth—
Well knowing I may not express the dearth
   Her death has made, as I could not define
  The loss if some flower, with which intertwine
The world's sweet thoughts, were blotted from the earth.

And yet we say : She gave us of her best ;
   Her heart was open as her eyrie home ;
    Her thought as if by mirrors multiplied.
And, standing by the red man of the West,
   She seemed like Justice on her mountain dome,
    Her pen a sword that flashed out far and wide.

NOT BY SELF-SIGHT.

NOT by self-sight, but by the Over-Sight,
  Shall we with safety journey to the end.
  As we progress, the landmarks veer and bend,
Nor boldest mariner may read aright
The lamps that glimmer in the live-long night
  On shores uncharted, never human-kenned ;
  By higher knowledge must we know our trend,
And lay our course off by an Inner Light.

The seasons draw the birds by night or day,
  Blindly the blossoms flower and fade and fall ;
    Are there not kindly seasons for the soul ?
What guide but Faith can show the unknown way,
  What ear but hers divine when wreckers call,
    While winds of God seek out the heavenly goal ?

SYMPATHY.

BY us she waits, unheralded and meek,
    Forgotten in the blessings that she brings ;
We do not guess her eyes conceal the springs
Of all the streams of gladness that we seek.
Until she wills, kind words we may not speak ;
    Without her hint the angels fold their wings ;
So soft her touch, and how for feeblest things
The smiles and tears run races on her cheek !

Lacking her counsel Love might go astray,
    And Charity itself would cast a chill,
        And Happiness on earth be but a name ;
Her golden key unlocks the poet's way,
    Else Genius, nathless all his mighty will,
        Might stumble blindly at the gates of fame.

WAITING.

AS little children in a darkened hall
    At Christmas-tide await the opening door,
  Eager to tread the fairy-haunted floor
About the tree with goodly gifts for all,
And in the dark unto each other call—
    Trying to guess their happiness before—
    Or of their elders eagerly implore
Hints of what fortune unto them may fall:

So wait we in Time's dim and narrow room,
    And with strange fancies, or another's thought,
      Try to divine, before the curtain rise,
The wondrous scene. Yet soon shall fly the gloom
    And we shall see what patient ages sought,
      The Father's long-planned gift of Paradise.

THE END.

119